Ages: 4–7
Grades: PreK–2nd

A Tad Too Much

(Don't Cry Wolf)

Written by K. Emily Hutta
Illustrated by Yakovetic Productions

Tad was on his first camping trip, and he was having the best time ever! He especially loved eating dinner sitting around a campfire.

2

"May I have another hot dog, please?"
Tad asked. "Coming right up," Dad said.

Then he handed Tad a hot dog just the
way Tad liked it, with tons of ketchup.

Tad took a big bite of his hot dog, and a big blob of ketchup fell right onto his overalls. Tad looked around at his family. No one had noticed.

GO

STOP

4

In the dim light of the campfire, the ketchup on Tad's clothes looked a lot like blood. And that gave Tad an idea.

"Owwww!" he yelled. "My knee! Help!"

Mom rushed over to Tad. Leap ran to get a bandage. Lily put her hands over her eyes.

"Let's see, Tad," Dad said, grabbing a flashlight. Dad shone the bright light of the

flashlight onto Tad's knee and saw . . . ketchup.

Tad laughed. "I tricked you," he said.

"That wasn't funny, Tad," his dad said firmly. "We thought you were hurt."

After the excitement had died down, Leap, Lily, and Tad sat by the fire and told each other ghost stories while Dad and Mom cleaned up. Off in the woods they heard a rustling sound.

"What's that?" Lily asked nervously.

"Probably a raccoon or an owl," guessed Mom.

"Or a bear," joked Leap, trying to scare his sister.

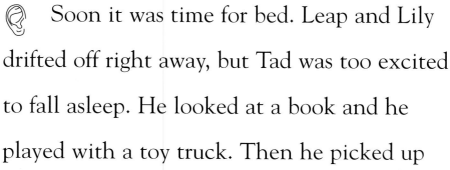

Soon it was time for bed. Leap and Lily drifted off right away, but Tad was too excited to fall asleep. He looked at a book and he played with a toy truck. Then he picked up

Leap's flashlight and began to fool around with
it. Its beam of light shone on his teddy bear,
casting a huge shadow on the side of the tent.
Tad couldn't resist playing a joke.

"Help!" yelled Tad. "It's a bear! It's going to get me!" Leap and Lily woke with a start just as Mom and Dad came running into the tent.

"Tad," Mom said, seeing that everything

was all right. "You never call for help unless you really need it!"

"Sorry," Tad mumbled. "I was just having fun."

The next morning, Mom and Lily went for a walk. Leap, Dad, and Tad decided to go down to the lake. Dad jumped in for a swim. Tad sat down next to his brother on the dock

and dangled his feet in the water.

"Leap, help!" Tad shouted suddenly.

"Something's got my foot, and it won't let go!"

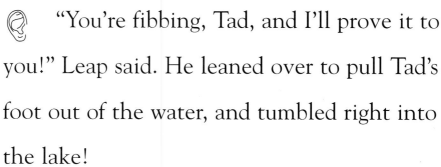

"You're fibbing, Tad, and I'll prove it to you!" Leap said. He leaned over to pull Tad's foot out of the water, and tumbled right into the lake!

"You fell for it!" Tad said, laughing. "Get

16

it? Fell for it? It's a joke."

    By this time, Dad had swum over to the
dock. Leap explained what had happened, and
Tad got a "time out" in the tent.

Later that afternoon, everyone was relaxing at the campsite. Tad was in the tent playing with his toy trucks.

"Tad," Mom called. "Do you want to

come out to hear a story?"

"Sure," Tad called from inside. Just then, the tent flap started to shake. "Hey!" Tad shouted. "I need help."

"Yeah, sure!" Leap said at the tent. "You're fibbing again!"

"No, really! I mean it this time," Tad shouted. He was sounding more frightened

20

now. "The zipper is stuck! I can't get out!"

"Tad," Dad said, "I would hope that you've learned your lesson by now."

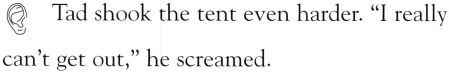 Tad shook the tent even harder. "I really can't get out," he screamed.

This time, Mom heard the panic in Tad's voice. She went over to the tent and pulled on the zipper. It was stuck, but it took her just a

22

moment to fix it.

"Why didn't you come sooner?" Tad asked,

hugging her tightly.

"Well, Tad, can you guess why?" Mom

asked kindly.

 "I pretended to need help too many times?" Tad asked.

"Right," Mom said. "So what have you learned?"

"Never cry for help unless you really need it," Tad declared, "and always bring a tent that has buttons!"